KID
CARAMEL™

PRIVATE INVESTIGATOR

P9-CQJ-663

E DUE

CASE OF THE MISSING
By Dwayne J. Ferguson

Just Us Books, Inc. • East

Printed in Canada
11 10 9 8 7 6 5 4 3 2
Library of Congress Number 96-75036

ISBN: 0-940975-71-8 (paperback)

Cover illustration copyright 1997 by Don Tate

He's Cool. He's a detective. He's a KID!

It was a typical day. Earnie and Caramel were headed to the art museum to check out the special exhibit: A Crystal Ankh, an icon from an African legend that has at last been found. A lot of other people show up to see the Ankh, too. And before anyone can say, "wow, that's pretty cool," the Ankh is gone.

But Caramel is on the case, He's already noticed that there are some pretty weird things going on at the museum. Things that probably shouldn't be going on – at *any* museum.

"Check this out, Earn ..." Caramel withdrew a plastic glove and a sandwich bag from his pouch. With the steady, unshaking hands of a heart surgeon, he carefully pulled at the fabric caught on the end of the glass ... inserted the material into the sandwich bag and sealed it tight. "Well, whoever our little thief is, he's clumsy. Earnie, see if you can find any more cloth. I'll search for other clues."

Chapter One —————

Earnest Todd never had it easy. The youngest of three brothers, he had become an expert at eating dirt, shining everyone else's sneakers, and making hand-me-down clothes look brand new. Now he was looking eye to fist at the bully of PS 40, Sharktooth Williams. Earnie reached into his pocket and offered Sharktooth two dollars not to beat his face into the ground. The combo platter of diplomacy and money worked almost all the time. At least it worked on humans (he hoped it would work on Sharktooth).

"Well, worm, whatcha gonna do about this chocolate milk stain on my shirt?" grunted Sharktooth, slime frothing from his mouth like a mad dog. A few gooey drops landed on his dirty gray sweatshirt.

The small crowd of fifth and sixth graders waited eagerly for the answer. Nothing was better than an after-school royal rumble on a warm spring day—well, except maybe for no school at all.

All eyes were on the trembling figure of little Earnie. The sweat dripping off his quivering forehead could have filled an Olympic-sized swimming pool.

"I s-said I was very very sorry and I'll pay for a new shirt—an extra large shirt—out of my allowance this week." Earnie whimpered like a frightened puppy. "Please don't knock my teeth out, Sharktooth!"

"You knew what you were doing, Todd!" Sharktooth yelled back. "You planned the whole little thing so nobody would think you're a wimp. Well, I got a newsflash for ya!"

Sharktooth grabbed the smaller boy's collar. "You *are* a wimp! Now you're gonna be like my favorite class—history!" Sharktooth laughed like a maniac in a horror movie, and he raised a massive fist that was armed to bring doom onto Earnie's head.

Earnie shut his eyes tight and let out a pitiful yelp as Sharktooth's fist headed for its target. Then, unexpectedly, the bully fell to the ground clutching his stomach in pain.

A familiar pair of white hi-top sneakers, which had yellow and blue hand-painted "K's" on them, headed toward a Earnest Todd who was highly relieved.

"I'm gonna start charging for being your bodyguard, Earn," smiled Caramel Parks. He placed a friendly hand on Earnest Todd's shoulder. Caramel was Earnie's best friend.

"Sooner or later, you're gonna have to punch Sharktooth in his jaw or he's gonna keep messin' with you," Caramel said.

"It's just that he's so much bigger than me, Kid. I'm really scared that one day he's gonna punch me into next week. Besides, I hate fighting. All it does is get a person beat up for nothing."

Using his sleeve, Earnie wiped the sweat from his brow. "But thanks for helping me out again. You know, I got a weekend job at my Aunt Daisy's candy shop. So I actually could *pay* you to be my bodyguard," said Earnie proudly.

"Uh, yeah, sure," Caramel said, brushing Earnie's idea aside. "But don't be surprised if I just stand by next time and wait for you to fight back." Caramel watched the other kids break up into smaller groups as they made their way toward the gates. "You should spend your fortune on Kupigana Ngumi lessons."

"I would if I knew what Nupigami Kguma was," replied Earnie.

"That's *Kupigana Ngumi*, Kid Caramel corrected his friend. "It's an African martial art. It's what Captain Africa uses in the comic books."

"Oh yeah! But while I'm learning Ngumi, you'd still help me out, right?" Earnie asked for reassurance but Caramel smiled sarcastically.

Earnie looked away, smiling. "You wouldn't do that to your best friend...would you, Kid?"

"That's what friends are for," Caramel replied. "Do you still want to check out the exhibit at the museum today?"

Earnie tilted his head proudly. "Since I'm the head reporter for the school newspaper, I think I do. Maybe I'll finally get some respect around here when everyone reads my super scoop on the legendary Crystal Ankh!"

"I never heard of it before I saw the flyers posted in the museum, but I can't wait to see it," Caramel said excitedly, "I mean it's worth like twenty million bucks! I could never save up that much allowance!"

"Ha!" Earnie laughed, "Especially as cheap as your father is!"

Caramel threw Earnie a false smile. "You're hilarious. Anyway, I'll bet you my dirt bike someone slimy tries to steal the Ankh."

"Wow, your dirt bike, Kid?" asked Earnie. His eyes brightened. He had always liked that bike and could see himself riding it as they spoke.

"Naw, I ain't bettin' you Kid because you're usually right. I'll be a hundred years old before I get a dirt bike," said Earnie.

"I wish I had twenty million dollars." A girl's voice came from behind a tree. Nikki poked her head out and flashed a huge lovey-dovey smile at Caramel. He suddenly felt seasick even though he was standing on dirt.

"H-hi...Nikki," said Caramel like he was about to barf. "No offense, but what do you want?"

She raced over to him and put her head on his shoulder. "I just wanna be around you. And I wanna know about that twenty million dollars you were talking about." She handed Caramel her bookbag.

"Earnie and I were talking about secret detective business, Nikki. We have to go now!" He placed her bookbag on the ground and pulled Earnie by the back of his shirt. "Let's get out of here."

The two boys walked out of the school playground. Behind them, a dirt-covered Sharktooth hurled mean looks as he walked out the gate on the opposite end. He pushed the other kids out of his way and huffed angrily to himself. "One day, Caramel Parks, I'm gonna make you wish you never heard of Sharktooth Williams. You'll see ... hahahahahahaahaaaahahaahaha!"

Chapter Two ———————

A little while later, the number twelve bus slowed to a screeching halt near the museum at the corner of Smith and Halby Streets. The brakes needed a major overhaul. Just about everyone on line to buy tickets for the exhibit covered their ears. The horrid death moans of the worn brake shoes were horrible to hear. After depositing several passengers, Caramel and Earnie included, the bus sputtered back into traffic, only to screech noisily again at the next corner.

Standing considerably taller than Earnie, Caramel could see that the line of ticket buyers stretched around the block. It wasn't every day that average people got the chance to see an object worth millions of dollars.

Caramel reached into his backpack for a piece of sugar-free-banana-flavored bubble gum. He was very health conscious, so he only chewed gum that was sugar-free. Banana flavor was his favorite, and he kept it in constant supply at all times. He claimed it helped him to think better, and as a detective that was big-time important.

"Would you like some gum, Earnie?" he offered, holding the yellow foil pack in front of Earnie's nose. It was amazing; it really did smell like bananas. Caramel was waiting for the day they invented steak flavor.

"Sure, thanks."

Watching Earnie chew gum was like looking at a rabbit tearing through a head of lettuce at a hundred miles an hour. It was a wonder he never bit his lip or tongue or that there was even any gum left when he was finished chewing on it.

Caramel sighed deeply. It did not seem as if the line was ever going to end. While he was waiting, Caramel opened his wallet and folded it over so his homemade aluminum foil Junior Detective badge was on top. It read:

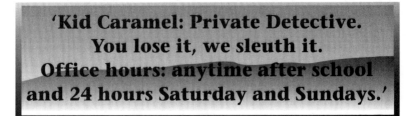

'Kid Caramel: Private Detective.
You lose it, we sleuth it.
Office hours: anytime after school
and 24 hours Saturday and Sundays.'

Now with his badge out, Caramel was no longer just an average boy next door. Nope, he was the Soon-To-Be-World-Famous-Boy- Investigator-Number-One, Kid Caramel. Unfortunately, he often got carried away and let his imagination take over. Way over.

One of his eyebrow's jumped up. His detective senses switched on. Problem number one: How to avoid the line? It was show time. To Caramel, the line stretched from here to Africa and only he could find a way to stealthily avoid it. Now he was detective and Ninja rolled into one.

"Looks like we're gonna have to pull some rank around here, Earn. Follow me." Kid Caramel held the badge over his head and waved it back and forth. "Excuse us, folks. This is official business. Beep beep, clear a path. Thank you."

The duo walked to the front of the line, ignoring the protests of the crowd. They marched into the side door. Earnie looked at his friend nervously.

"Uh, do you think it was smart cutting in line like that?"

"How old are we?"

"Ten."

"Look at that line. How many birthdays would pass by if we had stayed back there?"

"A million." Earnie finally smiled. Caramel pulled him to the window. There was an elderly person near the front of the line.

"See that old lady over there?" Caramel asked.

Earnie nodded.

"Well, she was ten when she got on line. Now look at her!" They chuckled for a minute until a security guard approached them.

"Hey, you two! How did you get in here?"

Kid Caramel flashed his Junior Detective's badge. The guard, whose own badge read "Jameson," did not find it particularly amusing. He waved his hand to his fellow officers, who were just down the hall. The three other guards joined him. The security guards gestured to the others. "This little kid's a cop on training wheels."

"Run along, children. This is serious business here. Cute badge, though. Now git!" The guards burst into laughter, but a sneer appeared on Caramel's face. He stared hard at the guards' uniforms. He was not just looking at the uniforms. He was using his spy eyes to magnify the

10

material, right down to the molecules! Suddenly his left eyebrow arched.

"Excuse you, Mr. Jameson, but you're talkin' to a detective, you know! If you ask around at the police department you'll notice I'm the one they call 'Kid Caramel.'"

"Ah, y-yeah...and I'm his official partner," added Earnie as backup.

Jameson leaned over. "Look, Kid *Camel*, you and your little friend here better high-tail it on home before I arrest you for disturbing the peace...and cutting on line!"

Kid Caramel and Earnie exchanged worried glances. Then Kid Caramel focused his attention on Jameson. He paused for a moment, thinking. "Let me speak with Captain Hutchinson, please. He'll let us in."

Jameson curled his lips as he answered. "Hutchinson won't be straightening anything out. Especially since his transfer to another department two nights ago. In other words, it's a long distance call to Alaska!" Again, all the guards laughed. Jameson slapped Kid Caramel on the back and turned him towards the door. The young detective mumbled the word 'transferred' to himself as he and Earnie landed outside onto the sidewalk. Reluctantly, they hopped back on line, only this time it seemed as if the line circled the Earth.

Kid Caramel rubbed his forehead. Something about the guards had bothered him, and he knew exactly what that something was. He had used his finely polished skills of deception on Jameson. There was no Captain Hutchinson. Caramel had invented the name to see whether the guards were real or not. He had never seen any of them before, and Caramel had visited the museum several times within the past few months to do homework. Not only that, but the uniforms the guards were wearing looked hand-dyed. Caramel stuck another piece of banana gum in his mouth.

He pulled Earnie close to his side and whispered in his ear. "Listen, something very strange is going on here and we have to figure out what it is. You with me?"

Visions of rude security guards pushing them out of tall windows flooded Earnie's mind. In short, he did not respond.

Then Caramel poked him in the ribs with his finger. "Earth to Earnie! Are you gonna help me or what? He explained to Earnie about the fake Hutchinson and tossed another piece of gum into his mouth.

Half an hour later, they reached the ticket window. To their surprise, they were still the same age. They paid the admission fee of two dollars and proceeded to the exhibit wing, the Spectral Room. Elaborately decorated walls, complete with gold trim, spanned majestically up to the thirty-foot-high ceiling. Overhead, the reflections from a crystal dome covered the ceiling in the center of the room. Blue and white tints from the sky and clouds illustrated an ever-changing picture in the sparkling glass. Eighteen Khemetic or Egyptian columns, like great oak trees, surrounded and added to the overall grandeur and wonder of the Spectral Room. This is where the museum displayed only the most spectacular exhibits.

Almost all of the tickets had been sold. The Spectral Room was getting a little crowded but Kid Caramel had no intentions of missing a single clue.

Standing by the whale-shaped punch fountain were the rich people. They were the kind that knew they were snobs, were proud they were snobs, and wanted the rest of the world to know they were snobs. Caramel made a mental note.

Next to the stage stood the parents and children, who bubbled with sincere excitement. Directly in the center of the room, near the veiled Ankh exhibit, were the politicians and other paper pushers. They were the type who tried to do the right thing but often did the easy thing instead.

A sudden loud blaring of instruments came from the direction of the stage. Kid Caramel was startled but he quickly regained his composure. The five-piece band played, or tried to play, their rendition of "Bad" by Michael Jackson. Caramel laughed and poked Earnie with his elbow. "Wow, this song *really* is bad...as in terrible!"

"Yeah, it's hurting my ears, it's so bad!" A thought hit Earnie. "Hey, Kid, did you notice the strange color of the uniforms the guards were wearing? They seemed bleached out, didn't they?" Earnie asked, feeling really proud that he may have picked up an important clue before the Junior Detective.

Unintentionally, Kid Caramel shattered Earnie's notion to tiny pieces. He removed a small notepad from his backpack. Scribbled on a page were the words "check out types of clothing dyes later. Uniforms were not the real deal."

Earnie frowned slightly, wondering when Kid had found the chance to write his notes and why he had not seen him do it.

Caramel leaned forward. "Yes, I noticed that. I also noticed that I didn't recognize any of the guards that were on duty." Before he could explain his observations to his friend, Mayor Greer tapped him on the shoulder.

"Kid Caramel! My, it's good to see you again, boy! And Earnest, Earnest, Earnest...how are you, son?" asked the elected leader of Tanwood. The Mayor was a slender fellow of six foot two, whose receding hairline kept trying to grow back as a toupee.

"I'm fine, sir," answered Caramel, smiling politely. He tried to keep his eyes anywhere but upward. He kept his gaze somewhere between the Mayor's bright yellow tie and his coffee-brown eyes.

"Me too, Mister Mayor, sir," added Earnie. He was quite nervous around anyone taller than himself, especially a living skyscraper like the mayor. He imagined that the toupee was really an alien that had attached itself to the man's head and was slowly sucking his brain juices through a straw. Earnie didn't know it but there was a really silly smile on his face.

"Calm down, son. I'm a friend," said Mayor Greer reassuring Earnie. "Oh, and speaking of friends, I'd like to introduce you fine young gentlemen to a very good friend of mine. He's the very man responsible for bringing the Crystal Ankh, not to mention tons of ticket money to our proud city. Haahaha!" The mayor motioned to his associate, who was finishing a glass of punch.

Tossing his cape to one side, the husky man placed his glass in the unsuspecting hand of a spectator, and strolled gallantly to the mayor's side. Caramel squinched his face in disgust. The Crystal Ankh's finder was just a bit too flamboyant for him.

"Check this guy out, Earn. He's got a cape!" Holding back his amusement, Caramel managed to straighten out his grin enough to look impressed.

Reaching for the approaching man's shoulder, the mayor pulled him into the small circle. "Caramel, Earnest, this is Prince Adbu of Pragi. Your highness, I present to you the famous boy detective, Kid Caramel and his associate, Earnest Todd."

Kid Caramel extended his arm to shake hands with the prince. Abdu of Pragi was in his late forties and wore a thick beard and mustache. Covering his forehead were deeply etched worry lines. He also had large bags under his eyes. You could go shopping with those bags, Caramel thought. The prince's outfit reminded him of a bad day in the life of Napoleon.

"Nice to meet you," Caramel said cordially.

"Likewise, young man," the prince returned with a royal tone.

"So, how did you find the Crystal Ankh, your Highness?" asked young Earnie with the sincerity of a lost lamb. He was gathering information for the school paper.

"That, my American friend, I shall most assuredly explain to everyone when I present my multimedia show on stage," His Highness replied with a foreign accent that Caramel could not quite place. It seemed stranger than anything else he had heard before.

"I will be going on in just five minutes, after our esteemed friend, Mayor Greer, introduces me to all of you," Prince Abdu answered.

The mayor looked around the room, and then at his watch. He nodded to the prince.

"Well, it looks like we may as well begin the festivities now, eh? I'll go up and introduce you now, Your Highness." With that, he disappeared into the crowd. Earnie watched the prince's assistant powder his face and shoot a blast of breath freshener into his mouth.

In a moment, Mayor Greer was on the stage. He was talking gibberish into the microphone to make certain it was working properly. "Ahem...testing...testing. Hello everyone and welcome to the Tanwood Museum. Today we celebrate a man and an ancient relic that is being viewed for the first time anywhere in the world."

Mayor Greer paused long enough for the audience to get the hint that they should start applauding. After an additional 'ahem' and the deliberate clearing of his throat, the crowd gave in and clapped wildly.

"Why, thank you for such an outpouring of love, citizens of Tanwood!" Now he waited for them to stop clapping.

"Not long ago, our guest heard of the legend of a special Ankh our African ancestors made of crystal ... but until now, no one has been able to find it. Well, that one individual is here among us in Tanwood. Ladies and gentlemen, boys and girls, I give you Prince Adbu of Pragi!"

Some people in the audience were thrilled to meet a real live prince. Others wanted to lay their eyes on the Ankh. But everyone applauded excitedly as the debonair royal highness took the stage in one amazing leap. Sticking his chest out and his chin up, the prince grabbed the microphone.

"Ahhh, my dear brothers and sisters. I humbly thank you so very much for having me here today and allowing me to share with you my prize...our prize."

19

To add a touch more of mystery to the event, he peered over the veiled display case, kept his eyes there, and waved his hand around. The audience started buzzing with anticipation. He decided to keep them in suspense a little longer. "You see, it is a long tale about how I came to find the Crystal Ankh. I will share with you the story through the wonderful world of multimedia." He waved his hand at a projection window high up in the north wall. "Tu'umba, play the tape please."

From the hidden booth, a gloved hand pressed a button, which dimmed the lights in the room and lowered the viewing screen to just a few inches above the stage.

Shortly the film rolled and the words "A Prince Adbu/Royal Splendor Film Works/ Production Joint" flashed across the screen. Silhouettes of excavation machinery stood out against the orange disk of the sun as it slowly descended from the heavens. Men dug deep into the earth with shovels, tossing dirt aside onto huge mounds. In the foreground Prince Adbu gave orders to the working men as they searched for the Crystal Ankh. The prince, dressed in khaki safari gear, walked to the camera. "As you can see, we have been working diligently from sunup to sunset. We are searching valiantly for the legendary Crystal Ankh, an elaborately sculpted symbol representing eternal life, power, prosperity, man, and woman. It was created by the Egyptians, known to themselves as the people of Khemite, which means 'land of the blacks.' The only other mystery surrounding the Ankh's whereabouts is which craftsworker sculpted it and which King or Queen commissioned the grand piece."

The film continued and the audience watched in amazement as the excavation team discovered a hidden temple beneath the sands. Then finally, after close to an hour, everyone cheered as the dust-covered prince emerged from the temple with the dazzling Ankh in his leather glove covered hands. "Because of its age and delicate nature, human hands cannot make contact with the crystal," explained the prince. "The oils from our fingers would only make the Ankh deteriorate that much faster."

The tape ended with a sneak preview of the aristocrat's next adventure. The screen read

"Coming soon...Prince Adbu and the Quest for Atlantis." The audience showed their enthusiasm with another thundering round of applause.

Caramel watched the film like everyone else, but he was also busy taking very detailed notes. One thing in particular caught his highly-trained hawk eye and really bothered him. Caramel didn't like it when he knew something was strange or out of place, and he couldn't put his finger on it. He sighed in frustration and looked up at the prince who had his hands up in victory.

The prince bowed and returned to the microphone. Again, he motioned to his assistant and a spotlight illuminated the veiled case. "Thank you gracious people! Thank you so much. It does my heart good to feel such warmth from my American friends." He placed a hand on the veil and curled his fingers beneath the thick blue and gold fabric. "And now, I present to you, the Crystal Ankh!"

He pulled the sheet away and suddenly a huge explosion from a smoke bomb rocked the room. Smoke and glass erupted from the stage.

The black smoke spread like fire and screaming people ran in every direction, knocking over other exhibits, trying to find the exit. Kid Caramel grabbed hold of Earnie's shirt to prevent him from straying into the hysteria and being trampled.

Coughing and rubbing his stinging eyes, Caramel pulled Earnie towards the stage. "Earn, are you OK?"

"I-I think so...what happened?"

"I don't know. Let's sit here until the smoke goes away."

After several long minutes of screaming and shouting, the cloud thinned into gray wisps and the commotion in the room calmed down somewhat. Caramel strained his red eyes toward the stage. He nudged his friend and pointed up at the shattered display case.

"Look, Earnie. The Crystal Ankh is gone!"

Chapter Three ─────────

The Tanwood Police were everywhere, like ants on a picnic basket. The museum was a writhing blanket of blue uniforms, mixed with flashing red lights that strobed through the shattered windows. The smoke had finally cleared and the visitors had been helped outside. Some of them had to be escorted to the hospital for minor cuts. In the middle of it all stood Kid Caramel and Earnie, who were slowly but surely being escorted themselves — straight out the door.

"But I'm telling you officer, I think I can solve this case!" Caramel exclaimed as he tried to wrench his arm from the vice-like grip of the police officer. He surely would have used his expertise in Kupigana Ngumi, had it not been a police officer.

"This is police business, kid, so leave this up to the police," exclaimed Sergeant Hayes, irritatedly. "Now go home!" the portly officer said. He was careful to mind his temper when dealing with kids. Officer Gene Hayes was in his late forties, eagerly looking forward to retirement, and not too thrilled by the prospect of baby-sitting. He was about to finally toss them to the curb when the glint of Kid Caramel's homemade badge caught his eye. Then the kid within himself broke through. Slightly.

"Say, is that a badge you've made for yourself?"

Caramel was stunned. What had happened to the hardened law man? With planned cunning, he could make the officer a pawn in his plan to obtain information. It was time for acting skills to take over. He turned on his wide-eyed 'baby face.' "Ah, y-yessir. I made it out of some recycled cardboard covered with aluminum foil. I'm planning on becoming a real live detective when I get out of college."

Hayes smiled. "I'm glad you're planning on going to college, young man. You're off to a good start by setting those kind of goals." He paused for a minute and looked around the room. He was the highest ranking officer on duty. Hayes tugged at both of the boy's shirts and snuck them back inside.

Earnie's eyes brightened. "You mean you're letting us stay?" He glanced at his friend with a mouth full of teeth and chewing gum. "He's gonna let us stay, Kid!"

"Ah, yeah...I heard. Isn't he great?" Kid Caramel straightened out his wrinkled shirt, thanked the officer, and reached for the notebook in his knapsack. Like a deer hunter, he sniffed the air, knelt to the floor to look for tracks, and forged ahead into the Spectral Room. Like a duckling, Earnie was right behind him.

Now the real work began: trying to make sense out of a few hundred shards of broken glass, wood, and cloth. Caramel was undaunted and completely determined to prove himself. He bit down on a fresh stick of banana gum and scribbled notes. Electrical sparks crackled in his brain as his clue-gathering supercomputer activated. He wrote tiny on purpose so only he, Earnie, and maybe an ant could read his notes. Even Captain Hayes could not make sense out of it, whenever he took a peek over Caramel's shoulder.

There was a large piece of broken glass dangling over a display case. It caught Kid's eye. He tapped his assistant on the shoulder and pulled him towards it. "Check this out, Earn...." He withdrew a plastic glove and a sandwich bag from his pouch. With the steady, unshaking hands of a heart surgeon, he carefully pulled at the fabric caught on the end of the glass. An overturned statue had fallen onto the glass, pinning it in place on the table. The material was blue, but it did not look as if blue was the original color. The edges were tattered as if someone had accidentally been caught on the glass, and had to deliberately destroy the shirt to get free. Kid Caramel inserted the material into the sandwich bag and sealed it tight. "Well, whoever our little thief is, he's clumsy. Earnie, see if you can find any more cloth. I'll search for other clues."

"Gotcha!"

Even though Earnie had only found a few clues in his stint as Caramel's sidekick, he was happy all the same that his friend had invited him to participate. That was what Earnie liked most about Caramel. He was a friend before anything else, dependable, trustworthy, and sincere. With great effort, the junior detective's second in command began his search.

Captain Hayes had returned to his officers and they continued their own hunt for clues. They had at their disposal all of the best criminalists Tanwood had to offer. Kid Caramel had just his wits, sincere intuition, determination, and an incredible sense of deduction to help him find the Ankh he and Earnie had waited so long in line to see.

To the police, it was just another job, another way to earn their pay. To Kid Caramel and Earnie, it was a search that would return a piece of their past, a piece of their heritage.

Chapter Four ─────────────

On the other side of town a lamp burned in bright shades of orange. It warmed up the corner of the room and provided light — just enough light to read the insurance claims form. The man leaned closer to his makeshift map, circling various points on the crumpled and faded paper for future reference. He knew now what he had to do. Nothing was going to stop him! The man glanced at the Crystal Ankh, its almost invisible surface glinting in the light of the lamp. The Ankh was well worth the trouble he had gone through to steal it. But there was one additional treasure the Ankh could bring that drove him to obsession. No one knew about the Ankh's little secret but him. And no one would find out. If they did, they would have to pay the price. A very, very nasty price indeed.

Suddenly, there was a thud at the door downstairs. The man hurled a heavy sack over the Ankh and blew out the flame inside the lamp, plunging the room into darkness. Only the slender yellow fingers of the moon's glow provided light. The man reached for his weapon and made his way down one small flight of stairs. He crept to the front door, aimed his weapon, and slid the metal hatch away from the peep hole. He saw no one. Determined not to share his valuable prize, he grabbed the doorknob, opened the door, and swung his weapon about, ready to take care of whoever it was. The wind howled angrily, slamming the empty garbage can against the door.

"So, that's what that was!" the man exclaimed, blowing out a sigh of relief . He wiped the small beads of sweat from his dirty brow. "A stupid trash can." To double check, the man stepped outside and circled the entire building. Every few seconds, the Ankh flashed in his mind. Greed had overcome him. All he could think of was his treasure. It would all be for him. He would not even share a drop with his own mother! But there were some people he had to pay off. A small wrapper that read "Dye-all" crunched under the sole of his shoe.

As he entered the building, the man reached into his back pocket for a book of matches. He struck one against the banister, and climbed the stairs. His shadow crept eerily beside him, reminding him of a scene from an old black and white movie. At the top of the stairs, the man made a left and kicked the bathroom door open. The pain in his arm would not go away. He noticed that it still bled slightly, even through the bandage. The theft was planned flawlessly, he thought, but even he could not avoid the shards of glass at the museum. The hydrogen peroxide stung a little but it was better than risking an infection. The man wrapped a fresh bandage around the wound and made for the room where his precious Ankh awaited. A crooked smile stretched across his face whenever he laid eyes on it. All to soon, he would be relaxing in the Caribbean sun on a seventy-foot yacht. Of course, that was after the limo ride to the airport and a first-class flight to the secret island. The FBI would never find him. It would go down in history as the crime of the millennium!

Chapter Five ————————

Caramel's fingers raced through the yellow pages until he found the word "Dyes." As he had guessed, there were not very many listings, only three to be exact. In his tiny secret handwriting, he jotted the numbers and addresses down on his notepad and returned the directory to the table. He checked his watch and decided it was much too late for any of the establishments to be open. It was nearing his bed time.

He reviewed the events of the day: the phony security guards, the torn piece of cloth, and now the phone numbers. He didn't really have concrete evidence to work with, but then that's how it always was in cases like these. You got lots of hoopla and pieces of a puzzle to put together, but no one piece of evidence that would make itself more noticeable than the others.

"Kid...Kid! I think I found something!" Earnie shouted from the Spectral Room. Caramel dumped everything into his knapsack, summoned his "cheetah speed," and dashed over to his friend. Earnie was kneeling under an oak table that supported an Oriental vase collection. Many of the vases had survived the explosion but there were tiny cracks in a few of the smaller ones. Earnie was scooping a handful of tiny white hairs into his palm. "I think this is rabbit fur." He offered it to Caramel with a monstrous smile.

"Great job, Earn!" Kid congratulated his friend sincerely. "The funny thing is, it's spring time, so who would be wearing rabbit fur?"

Like a Ninja, Sergeant Hayes appeared behind the boys. Caramel was impressed yet annoyed. His own razor-sharp hearing hadn't alerted him to the Sergeant's presence. He'd have to work on that. Hayes was pointing to his watch. "Time to go beddy-bye, guys. Or your parents will never let me hear the end of it." He craned his neck to see the ball of fluff in Caramel's hand. "Whatcha got there?"

"Earnie found what looks like rabbit hair." Caramel handed the officer a portion. "Maybe your science lab could run some tests on it. I have a microscope in my high-tech lab at home, so I'm going to be making my own analysis. Maybe we can compare notes tomorrow."

Hayes's eyebrow rose in amusement. This kid was serious. "Ah, sure. Maybe we'll do that." He escorted them to his squad car and dropped the kids off at their homes. Caramel told Earnie that he would start to study the evidence when he got in (after his parents fell asleep) and would let Earnie know everything the next day in school.

@@@@@@@@@

Before the school bell could finish its irritating ring, Kid Caramel and Earnie were heading to the police station on the #12 bus. Once again, it was detective time, and they had the perfect undercover vehicle. What thief would expect a world-class detective and his humble side-kick to travel on a lowly bus?

"I have a primary suspect in this case, Captain," reported Caramel confidently as he and Earnie stepped into his office. "But I'm going to need the police department to help stage a new exhibit at the museum."

"Oh, really," Captain Hayes said sarcastically.

"I know who the thief is," Caramel replied

assuredly. "I've studied this case, and I can solve it."

Captain Lucas stared at the boy. It was quite obvious there was more to the Kid than met the eye. Captain Lucus bit his lip with curiosity and nodded.

"What is your plan?" he asked casually.

The junior detective pointed to his friend. "Earnie here works at his aunt's candy shop. They make candy gifts like sculptures, displays, you name it. I have an idea that might help us trap this cunning thief once and for all. We can smoke him out by making him think he has a fake Ankh."

"You may have something, Kid. Let's take this to my superiors."

"Sounds good so far," replied the Captain. "Fill me in on the details and I'll see what me and my boys can do for you."

Caramel and Earnie exchanged smiles. "Thanks, Captain," Caramel said. He opened the door to leave the office and couldn't resist having one last word.

"By the way, be ready to catch a really big rat."

Chapter Six

It was close to midnight when the van pulled up to the newsstand. A shadowy figure stepped out and dashed into the little store. The man plunked his quarter down on the counter and folded the newspaper. Then he tucked the paper under his arm, grabbed the cup of coffee, a few extra sugars, and some creamer. Outside, the crisp rain patted gently on the sidewalk and the man headed for his van. With a yank, the door popped open. He sat down on a pile of old magazines and empty bags of potato chips.

He turned to the front page of his newest paper. First, his eyes skimmed the weather information in the upper left-hand corner. Then they landed on the first headline, a story about politics, as usual. "Who cares?" he whispered to himself. Then his eyes and heart stopped cold. This was totally impossible. His immediate reaction was to take another look, to hope he was seeing things. The headline read:

Crystal Ankh Found!
New exhibit scheduled for Saturday

The article began:

Once believed stolen, the legendary Crystal Ankh, discovered in northern Africa by famed archaeologist Adbu, has been recovered by the authorities of the Tanwood area. Now, top re searchers have agreed that the original Ankh, the one stolen, was indeed a phony, and that the genuine artifact has been found.

The man crumpled up the paper and threw it angrily into the back seat. With a huff, he turned the ignition and stomped the gas pedal to the floor. The van pulled off with a loud squeal and acrid smoke mixed with the rain.

The only thoughts on his mind were those concerning his Ankh. How could it be, the man astonishly wondered. Someone must have been watching him. Yes, that's it! When he snuck out for the morning paper, they snuck in and took the Ankh. They would pay dearly. The Ankh was his and no one else's. Didn't they know how much he had worked planning to steal it? Didn't they appreciate the countless hours he had put into planning the crime of the millennium? It wasn't easy, the man thought. He almost hit a couple of pedestrians as he ran a light. The drive seemed unbearably long. What normally took a little while stretched on for centuries in his mind.

I thought I stole the original Ankh! Now how will I complete my plans? The fake will not do! My contacts won't pay me for a fake Ankh, he thought as he turned the corner into a wooded area.

Finally the weed-covered walls of the abandoned factory he had come to know as home spread across his windshield. But the anxiety in his heart only grew more intense. The headlights of the van dimmed to a cool yellow, then went black. There were no lights outside his hideout, except for the mild glow from the street lamps. The man bounded up the staircase, taking four steps at a time. He tore the protective blanket from his treasure like a man gone mad. It still looked real to him, but the mind could be tricked by words. The article had done its damage. This Ankh was no longer the real thing to him. "They" wouldn't pay him for the theft! A tear rolled down his cheek and he slid onto his calendar from a stack of books. With a thin red marker, he circled Saturday and sketched a picture of a dagger in the box marking the fateful day.

Chapter Seven

It was as close to perfect as Caramel and Earnie had ever seen. Aunt Daisy grinned and rolled up her sleeves. "Well, Earnie, what do you think of your old auntie now?" She pointed to the secret weapon that would catch the thief. The thin wrinkles at the edge of her eyes curved up with her wide smile.

"You're still the best artist in the family, Aunt Daisy," he beamed in appreciation. She was his favorite aunt. Aunt Daisy was so much fun to be around. She always did impersonations of movie stars and could tell the funniest stories in town. He stood in the middle of the candy shop daydreaming. Now she would reach legendary status in Tanwood, thought Earnie, and probably the earth. Better than that, Earnie would be known as her favorite nephew.

"Well, Earn...we've got to get this to the museum. Caramel congratulated Aunt Daisy for her fine work and punched his partner lightly in the back. Earnie could dream, and it sometimes took a rock to the side of the head to snap him out of it. "Earth to Earnie.... Hellooooooooo!"

"Huh? What?" Earnie's glazed over eyes returned to normal as reality sunk back in. Caramel's face came into focus. His friend did not look happy. Earnie turned to his aunt and spoke. "Oh, yeah...we'd better get going. Thanks, Aunt Daisy. I'll make sure to give you a big write up in the school paper for your help!"

"Anything for you, Earnie. Now do your auntie proud and catch that weasel." Daisy covered the secret weapon in protective bubble wrapping and gently laid it inside a wooden box. Then she sealed it tight with several strips of thick shipping tape. She gave the boys the thumbs up and walked them to the door. "Good luck detectives." She winked and waved until the police car was out of sight.

There were flyers posted all over Tanwood: See the REAL Crystal Ankh. Free admission to those with old ticket stubs. It seemed that the Tanwood residents were more excited than before. Unfortunately, the real residents of Tanwood were to find out that the new exhibit was off limits for this showing.

Police Captain Lucas rounded his officers up in the briefing room. "This new exhibit is by invitation only," he pointed to the elaborately designed invitations. "And guess who's invited? That's right, you are. Everyone available will be going in undercover as the citizens of Tanwood. You will become lawyers, doctors, plumbers, sanitation workers, and teachers. We will catch the suspect, who shall remain unnamed. And I'll tell you exactly why he will remain unnamed. If you officers know who we're looking for, it will be that much harder to hide the fact that you're undercover. Only three people will know: Caramel Parks, his friend Earnest, and I." He gave Caramel the OK to take the podium.

"Hi." Caramel was confident yet a bit nervous. There were over forty officers looking dead in his face— officers who still could not believe they were working on a grand-theft case with a child. Caramel looked at the crowd once more. Some of them were ready with notepads. Others were frowning. Kid swallowed to wet his suddenly dry throat. He then made a mental note to brush up on his public speaking skills. "Um, here's the plan." Caramel began to fill them in on the details when he was interrupted by several officers clearing their throats, yawning, laughing, and shuffling. He turned to Captain Lucas for help. Lucas simply gave him a look of encouragement and shot a patented mean look at his officers. They straightened up immediately as if being addressed by the Shaka, King of the Zulus, himself. Caramel continued...."and that's how we'll catch him. Thank you."

Up stepped Captain Lucas. "There you have it men, nothing more, nothing less. You have your assignments so let's catch us a criminal!"

Chapter Eight ─────────

Saturday morning arrived on the whistle of the six o'clock train and the sound of cartoons on TV's across town. Caramel had found the night before almost impossible to sleep through. He had tossed and turned the entire night as if it was the night before Christmas. Caramel hopped out of bed at the first ray of sunlight and raced down the stairs into the kitchen where he gulped down two huge bowls of Frosty Wheat Puff Bombs with marshmallows. Just as quickly, he ran back up to his room and dressed. Much to his surprise, his mother, Elizabeth, was standing in his closet. He dreaded the thought of what she was doing.

"Morning, Caramel. I think you'd look really cute in this outfit." She held up a pair of pants, socks, a shirt and a light baseball jacket. Then she held up the cap. A cold chill ran down his spine. Everything matched like the clothes came straight out of a catalog. Guys tried not to match on purpose! Worse than that, he hadn't worn any of those items for over two years. With a half smile-half-frown, he put his hands up over his head.

"You're the best mom in the world, but I'm big enough to dress myself."

"Oh, I know that. But today is your big day and I thought you might need an extra hand." Her sincerity was angelic. But she understood. All guys eventually have to grow up. She stepped to the side and sat at the edge of his bed. Caramel was relieved but also felt as if he was leaving nothing for his mother to do. She hadn't seen him eat breakfast, so an idea flashed in his head. He rubbed his stomach.

"Boy, I sure could use one of your world famous eat-til'-you-drop pancake breakfasts. The kind where you eat so much, you can see the food through your eyeballs."

"My baby's hungry?"

"I could eat an elephant's family." Through the closet mirror, he glanced over his shoulder. His mother had a look of pure joy on her face. She hopped off the bed and was on her way out of the room.

"How many pancakes would you like? Two, as usual?"

He put his finger on his jaw in thought. "Nah, I think I should go for three and a half today. And a couple of sausages, too." He giggled at the sound of his mother skipping down to the kitchen. She was humming one of those songs she said she used to dance to when she was a teenager. Those songs never had raps in them, but they did have some cool beats, Caramel thought to himself.

Breakfast was incredible. Mom had put extra love into each and every pancake, sausage, egg, and hash brown. Caramel's stomach felt like it would explode if he even breathed the wrong way. But sometimes being a son meant going the extra mile for the one person who loves you more than anything in the world.

Caramel's father, Ronald, strolled into the kitchen like a bear just emerging from hibernation. He was a big man of six foot five and a hefty 220 pounds of pure muscle. Well, almost pure muscle. Pancakes and good home cooking did tend to make mister stomach a wee bit on the round side. "Smells good, Liz. Mornin' son." His eyes examined the boy's plate. "Looks like you just discovered food for the first time, boy."

46

"Good morning, Pop. I'm just growing again, I guess." He pointed to the food. "I even left a little bit for you." The trio shared a warm laugh and soon his mother and father began to eat breakfast themselves. His father poured himself a tall glass of grapefruit juice and pounced on the last two pancakes like a lion.

"So, your mother tells me you're going to catch a thief today." Mr. Parks said. He was an entertainment lawyer and often worked long and late hours. Although his lovely wife kept him up to date on Caramel's adventures, he still wanted to be an active part of his son's life by helping wherever he could. No sooner had he finished the sentence, Caramel's little sister, Tasha, walked into, or rather rolled into the kitchen. She was "driving" the bright yellow plastic sports car she'd received on her fifth birthday. She crashed into her mother's chair with a light thud.

Caramel chuckled and answered his father. "Yes, sir. We're gonna nab the person who stole the Crystal Ankh with a secret weapon. I can't wait!"

"I'd like to speak with Captain Lucas before you go back to the museum. I want you to understand that this could be dangerous and I want to make sure everything is planned perfectly before you do this."

Caramel frowned. "Aw, Pop, I know what I'm doing."

"You're a smart boy, Caramel. But I want you to be safe. Even the best crime fighters put as much energy into staying safe as they do to catch the bad guys. You understand me?" he said sternly. He reached over the table and rubbed the top of his son's head.

"I understand. If I'm going to be the world's greatest detective, I have to be twice as smart as the bad guys. I'll be in my room until you finish talking with Captain Lucas. I'm gonna go over my notes one more time."

"We'll see you in a little while," said his mother. She picked Tasha up out of her car and fixed a small bowl of oatmeal for her. The little girl sipped on a cup of juice while her meal was prepared. She looked at her daddy with a look of determination in her eyes.

"I'm gonna be a 'tective, too!"

He shook his head playfully and sighed. "Here we go again, Liz."

Earnie's parents pulled away from the museum in their station wagon after saying their good mornings to Caramel's folks. Caramel stepped out of his parent's car and watched them pull away too. It was comforting for the boys to know that both sets of parents would be watching the events on video cameras downtown in the Tanwood Police Headquarters (even though they'd never admit it).

Since this occasion was to be "by invitation only" there was a very short line. The security opened the doors fifteen minutes late to put added pressure on the suspect. Kid knew that when things did not go exactly as planned, criminals made mistakes. Everyone filed into the room in a orderly fashion. To make it seem legitimate, several officers even brought their children along. It would look odd if Caramel and Earnie were the only kids present.

Mayor Greer personally greeted everyone and directed them towards the refreshments. His eyes searched the crowd for any strangers but he knew everyone so far. The last people to arrive were Prince Adbu and his assistant Tu'umba.

They mingled with the crowd and the aristocrat happily signed any autographs requested of him. Prince Adbu flagged down the Mayor. "My friend, Mayor Greer, I was wondering," he scanned the room himself, then lowered his voice to a whisper, "have you seen you- know-who?"

Mayor Greer finished a shrimp appetizer and washed it down with punch. He also whispered, "You mean the thief? I have no idea who he or she may be. But we do have a heavy security team." Several uniformed officers surrounded the room. The officers surveyed the room, taking extra care not to let on that they recognized their fellow officers. "Are you ready to present the real Ankh?"

"Yes, although I am embarrassed. Someone obviously switched the real one the night before my original presentation. I hope the audience will understand."

"I'm certain they will, Your Highness." The Mayor asked his assistant for the cordless microphone. He glanced around the room until he saw Kid Caramel. He winked and took the stage. "Ah, ladies and gentlemen. I am so pleased that you were able to return here to the elegant Tanwood Museum for the showing of the real Crystal Ankh. On behalf of the Tanwood Historical Community Programming Committee, I apologize for the inconvenience. Now, without further ado, I am proud to present to you, the individual who originally discovered the Crystal Ankh, Prince Adbu.

Once again, thunderous applause filled the room. Prince Adbu graciously accepted the microphone and bowed. "Ladies and gentlemen of Tanwood. I am humbled by the fact that you have paid your hard-earned money to see such a precious relic. You were cheated and still came out with open arms and hearts. I want you to know that I too have been wronged. Someone has taken advantage of my hard work and taken from us a piece of our culture. It has been found, fortunately. And most of all, I am once again most honored to present it to you." It was like an instant replay to Kid Caramel and Earnie, watching the multimedia presentation and hearing the long drawn out tale again. Caramel wondered if the explosion would also happen at the same time and in the same way. It would make things much easier.

Unfortunately, that was not the case. The prince finished his presentation and began taking questions from the audience. Ten minutes passed before the prince wrapped up the show. Now the audience was invited to view the Crystal Ankh. This time, there wasn't a protective glass case surrounding the Ankh. A single-file line was formed and one by one the guests were allowed to enter the roped security area.

This time the explosion came from a small statue that was in the hallway next to the viewing line. Since there was no glass casing around the Ankh, no one was injured with deadly shards. Once again smoke filled the room and it made Kid Caramel's lungs itch. He heard someone running toward the door. He yelled at the top of his burning lungs, "Now!" The front doors slammed shut and the running footsteps quickly changed direction. They went down to the lower level.

Several officers were coughing uncontrollably. Even though the officers' children had been given instructions on what to do if there was another smoke bomb, they still scrambled about noisily. It was Earnie's job to round them up and to calm them down.

Caramel and five officers ran downstairs and entered the lower level with caution. All of the doors had been secured. It was just them and their suspect. There was nowhere to go. Unfortunately, they were in a museum so there were definitely plenty of places to hide. And, if the suspect was the same person who had stolen the Ankh the first time, he would know the museum's layout by heart.

Captain Lucas tried the lights. The power had been shut off. He then ordered his electrical technician to get to work on restoring the power. The officer jumped to the job right away, feeling his way to the fuse box. He had quite a few tools on his belt and began to tangle with the cut wires.

Kid Caramel shouted into the darkness of the room. "I know who you are! I have fur from your gloves!" He squinted his eyes, trying hard to see anything. "There's only one person who would try to fool everyone that you had to wear gloves to touch the Ankh." The room was pitch black. He put his hands out in front of his as he walked deeper into the basement.

Suddenly footsteps raced toward him and a hand reached around the collar of his shirt. The hand yanked Caramel into the darkness. He shrieked in surprise and fear. "Help me! He's got me!"

Captain Lucas withdrew his flashlight. He carefully aimed the light from one part of the room to another. "Smith, how are we coming with those lights?"

"Almost got it, sir!" the electrical specialist replied from the far corner of the room.

Kid Caramel bit the man's fingers with everything he had. The man yelled angrily in pain and Caramel squirmed free. "Shine your lights over here. Over here!" Suddenly the left corner of the room was flooded with light and the officers readied themselves for any wrong moves.

"Freeze!" Captain Lucas shouted with authority. When he saw the suspect, his eyes opened wide. Caramel was right!

Kid Caramel opened the plastic bag that held the rabbit fur. He scooped the fur up and tossed it at the suspect. "I think this belongs to you. I studied your video tape presentation at the museum. You had gloves on. The same gloves in your multimedia presentation....Prince Adbu! Otherwise known as Benny Hodegman, gas station attendant and wanted criminal in fourteen states. You're also a makeup specialist who was a stage designer in college. I liked your set of Africa, by the way. The temple actually looked real."

The phony aristocrat held the phony Ankh protectively against his chest with one arm. "How did you figure that out? You're just a stupid kid."

"You didn't do your homework. You said in your video that you had to wear gloves to prevent oil from your fingers from damaging the crystal. Well, there's oil in leather gloves, too! That told me you were a fake. Too bad your story about it's theft won't get you the insurance money now."

The bogus prince reached behind his back, searching for a weapon. His hand bumped into knight's suit of armor. He grabbed its sword and waved it back and forth defensively. "S-stay back all of you! That insurance money is mine, all mine! I'll do whatever I have to keep it. I saved my money from the gas station for years to have the Ankh made. It cost me everything I had. Everything! I won't let you ruin years of planning! All I have to do is get rid of all you witnesses!"

"Very clever, Benny," said Caramel. "You spent a few thousand to have the Ankh made, took out a large insurance policy on it, created a fake set of Africa and the guise of a prince, stole your own ankh, and waited to get paid."

Benny swung the sword too hard and the blade stuck itself into a wooden crate. It was the break Caramel had been waiting for and he kicked Adbu in the knee, forcing the "Prince of Pumping Gas" to fall. The candy Ankh sprung from his hands and he screamed in horror as it spiraled through the air, barely missing the ceiling. Caramel leapt into the air and caught it just before it hit the ground.

"Tell us where the insurance policy is or I'll smash the Ankh." Caramel held the fake artifact over his head.

"Noooo!" Benny yelled in panic. "Please, you can't. It is worth a fortune."

"Oh well, I guess you're gonna have to really go to a desert temple to find another Ankh."

He prepared to throw it.

"All right. All right, I'll tell you where the policy is..." the criminal cried in defeat. He gave the police the address to the abandoned warehouse as they handcuffed him. They led him outside and into an awaiting squad car. Caramel ran to the vehicle.

"By the way, your Highness," he smashed the Ankh against the sidewalk and it shattered into a million tiny sugar cubes. If you had put your money where your mouth is, you would have noticed that this Ankh was made of candy. Maybe my partner's aunt will send you some more to help you enjoy your stay in prison!"

Chapter Nine

After all of the excitement of the past few days, Caramel and Earnie had grown accustomed to crowds. This crowd, however, was full of reporters. Today, the Mayor of Tanwood would present the boy detectives with a special honor. The festivities were held in the auditorium of Tanwood PS #1.

"May I have your attention please," Mayor Greer asked politely. He took both Caramel and Earnie by the shoulders and nudged them to the front of the stage. The boys smiled nervously as the photographers snapped dozens of photos for the local newspapers. They saw their parents in the audience and felt reassured by their support. The Mayor continued, "Today I am very proud to present these two young sleuths with these honorary gold detective badges from the Tanwood Police Department. Caramel's eyes popped wide open as he was given the badge. It even came in a leather case just like real detectives. The boy genius took the microphone.

"Thank you to everyone at the Tanwood Police Department. I want to thank my mom and dad for their support and Captain Lucas for letting me help. But most of all, I wanna thank my best friend on the planet Earth, Earnie." He patted his buddy on the back and faced the crowd again. "Oh, and no more aluminum foil badges for me!"

"Yeah, whatever he said," Earnie added with a shaky grin. He winked at his parents as he accepted his badge. "By the way, from now on, you can call me Kid Earnie."

Caramel grabbed the microphone with a big smile. "I don't think so." He pushed Earnie away from the podium and gave him a hearty handshake. "How about we celebrate with a big ice cream sundae?"

Earnie grinned. "Sure. It doesn't take a detective to know that's a great idea!"

The Beginning

Tell Us What You Think About
KID CARAMEL!™

Name _____

Address _____

City_____ State ____ Zip _____

Birthdate _____ Grade _____

Teacher's Name _____

Who is your favorite character in this book? Do **you know**
of anyone with a personality like Caramel? **Or Earnie?**
_____

Write down the title of this book.
_____

What topics would you like to see treated in **future KID**
CARAMEL™ books? _____
_____

How did you get your first copy of KID CARAMEL™?
Parent? Gift? Teacher? Library? Other?
Are you looking forward to the next title in **this series?**
Why or why not? _____
_____
_____

Any other comments? _____
_____

Send your reply to:
KID CARAMEL™ c/o Just Us Books, Inc. 356 **Glenwood**
Avenue, East Orange, NJ 07017